WEiRDo 2

EVEN WEIRDER!

Text copyright © 2014 by Anh Do
Illustrations copyright © 2014 by Jules Faber

ISBN 978-1-338-30560-9

10 9 8 7 6 5 4 3   19 20 21 22 23

Printed in the U.S.A.   23
This edition first printing 2019

Typeset in Chaloops Senior, Push Ups, and Lunch Box

BLAH,
BLAH,
BLAH

ANH DO

Illustrated by JULES FABER

WEiRDO 2

EVEN WEIRDER!

SCHOLASTIC INC.

I was out shopping for a **birthday present** for the seventh-best-looking girl in the class. So why did I have five years' worth of **toilet paper** in the cart?

Because

my life is
weird.

If something's on sale at the store, Mom will buy <u>lots</u> of it.

And guess what was on sale today?

That's right,

toilet paper.

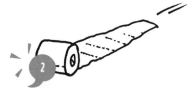

There we all were . . . looking like

the family that has the

MOST POOS

in the world.

The fact is, we don't just use toilet paper in the bathroom. We use it for other **stuff** around the house . . .

Like **blowing** your nose.

Wiping up **spills**.

escapee!

Ten pin bowling.

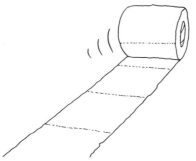

Did I tell you my mom was **thrifty**? She's one of those people who gets a little too excited about the lady in the corner of the shop giving out the free sausage samples.

SMILE!

Mom will make us **all line up** for a taste, no matter what the sample is.

BROCCOLI BALLS?

YUMMO!

DUCK DONUT?

WOW WEE!

You're only allowed **one** sausage per person, but Mom makes us walk away and then come back looking slightly different, just to get **more food**.

And if the sausages are **REALLY** tasty, she'll make us come back one **extra time**.

GREAT!
NOW WE DON'T HAVE TO WORRY ABOUT LUNCH!

Roger's **the worst** at shopping. Somehow **strange stuff** always ends up in the cart when he's around.

WHO BOUGHT THESE CHIPS AND JUMBO SAFETY PINS?

guilty

WHO BOUGHT THIS ITCHY BUTT CREAM?

guilty

10

Anyway, there we were at the checkout with our

2,000

rolls of toilet paper, when I looked across and saw . . . BELLA ALLEN!

HI, WEIR!

HI, BELLA.

"What are you buying?" she asked.

"We're just buying a . . . birthday present for you," I replied.

"Is that my present behind your back?" she asked with a smile.

"Oh, no, that isn't for you either."

I brought out the itchy butt cream to show her.

SEE? THIS IS JUST, UMM, JUST IN CASE . . . CHEAP TOILET PAPER CAN BE A BIT ROUGH SOMETIMES!

ITCHY BUTT CREAM

What was I saying?!

"Okaaaaay, bye, Weir," she said.

Nooooo!

Now Bella Allen thinks I am **the king of poop**. That I need a cart full of toilet paper all for myself!

Can my life get any **worse?**

My life just got worse!

Now the **whole** supermarket's looking at me!

How did the lady at the checkout know my name? Must have been

a lucky guess!

CHAPTER 2

My first name is **Weir**. My last name is **Do**. (Yep, rhymes with "go.")

Just in case you missed my first book, let me tell you a little bit about me and my family.

Dad

Mom (thrifty)

Granddad

Me

Roger

Sally

toilet paper

You already know I'm a **bit weird**. Like when they handed out **talents**, I wound up with . . .

And when they handed out family hobbies . . .

And you already know that my mom is thrifty. She **really** is.

For **Roger's birthday**, instead of paying for **real** helium balloons that float up to the ceiling . . .

. . . she just blew up plain balloons and then **stuck** them to the ceiling with **sticky tape**.

She's also one of those moms who makes us wear **hand-me-down** clothes. I got stuck with Sally's **old school shoes** . . . but at least I didn't get her sweater!

My sister, Sally, is **super** neat. She does

everything
perfectly.

She even peels an orange all in **one go**.

perfect

And she's really good at making things,
like **balloon** animals.

orange
peel

Sally **never** makes
a mess eating her
noodles.

But me, I always seem to get that one long noodle that goes on and on forever!

At least I'm not as **messy** as Roger. Sometimes he even ends up with noodles **coming out of his nose**.

Roger is my little brother, and he likes to **destroy stuff**. This week he's been **throwing** things into the bath. To "**clean**" them.

Often important things . . .

CLEAN!

Mom refused to waste the soggy bread . . . and I have to say, the **soggy sandwich** was one of the **worst three sandwiches** I've ever had in my life.

soggy sandwich

2nd worst sandwich (carrot and tomato)

number 1 worst sandwich ever (pig ears)

My dad is just plain strange.

He can do a burp that lasts for a looooooooooooooooooooooooooooooooooooooooooooooooong time!

27

uUURRR

still going!

finally finished!

Dad can also **fart** from the **front door** to the **back door**, but we won't go into that.

The other thing Dad likes to do is **dance really badly**. He tries to copy people on TV.

horsey dance

worm dance

robot dance

← still the
worm dance →

33

Finally, there's Granddad. His teeth come out, and his body parts make **funny** noises . . .

WHOOP WHOOP!

And he likes to play **silly** tricks.

《SHAKE》 HANDS?

ZZZZZ
ZZZZZ
ZZZZZZ!

HA HA
HA HA HA

35

He also pulls his pants up really high, which is the opposite of some of the cool kids at school.

Granddad—
high

Joey Keenan—
low

Toby Hogan—
super
low

Even our pet bird is weird. Most birds like to make happy chirpy noises. But Blockhead always makes strange sounds, like . . .

WOOF
WOOF!

And sometimes . . .

MOOO!

And if he's eaten some funny birdseed, he'll say . . .

WANNA
FIGHT?

Henry's my best friend from school. He doesn't care that I'm weird, or that I like to draw silly pictures.

Like this one . . .

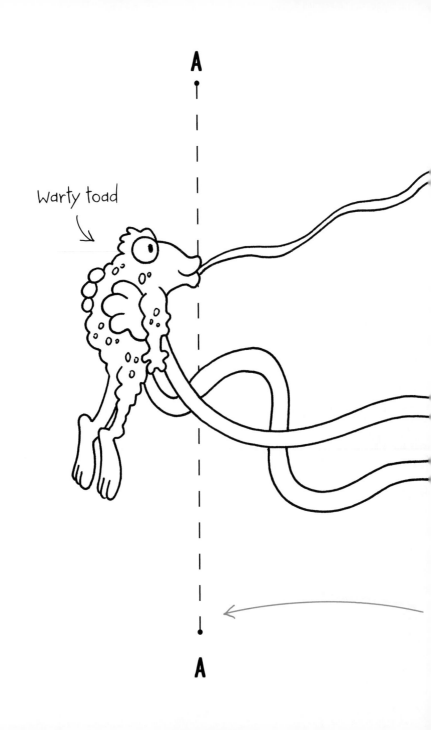

Warty toad

A

A

B

Blake

Fold line B over
to meet line A

B

Me and Henry like to make up new words for things, too . . . like **"Finkles."**

That's the word we invented for the **wrinkles** you get on your **fingers** when you've sat in the bath

for

too

long.

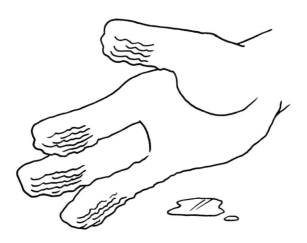

We think if we say it enough everyone will start
to use it,

even the queen.

CHAPTER 3

Bella's party is two days away, so I want to be as normal as possible at school to make sure that she won't un-invite me.

This was going to be hard since today we were going on a school trip to the **zoo** and Granddad was coming as a teacher's helper.

I knew it was going to be **trouble** when Granddad showed up at breakfast wearing fake **monkey ears**.

When we got on the **school bus**, Granddad took the empty seat next to Henry, and the only seat left for me was next to . . .

Bella.

I like Bella. I like her **a lot**. But I'm not sure if I'm ready to sit next to her on the bus.

We said hi . . .

HI, BELLA

HI, WEIR!

. . . and that's it!

I didn't know what else to say to her. She didn't know what else to say to me. We just sat there **staring** at the back of the heads of the people in front of us!

Henry

Granddad/ monkey

The sight of Granddad's **monkey ears** and Henry's **fuzzy orange hair** gave me an idea.

I took out my sketchbook and started **drawing** . . .

"What are you drawing?" Bella asked.

IT'S A MONKEYLION!

Bella reached down into her bag and pulled out a pair of **glasses**. She put them on and looked closely at my drawing.

HA! IT'S FUNNY.
YOU'RE A GOOD
DRAWER, WEIR.

I hadn't seen Bella wearing glasses before, and I must have been staring at them, because she noticed.

"The glasses are new," said Bella. "The eye doctor said I need to wear them when I'm looking at something closely."

"Cool," I said. "Can I try them on?"

SURE

She took them off and put them on me.

The glasses made **everything** look different.

They made Granddad's ears look

even bigger.

And Henry's head was HUGE!

You **do not** want to know what Toby Hogan looked like . . .

That was when Bella
asked me to **draw** her.

**WEIR,
CAN YOU
DRAW ME?**

YES!

This was my chance to **impress** Bella with
the one thing that I'm
really good at!

I picked up my sketchbook and pencil and
started drawing Bella as well as I could.

When I finished, I showed her the picture
of herself.

THAT'S . . .
  UMM, NICE,
WEIR . . .

Bella said it was nice, but I don't think she meant it, because she had the same look on her face that Mom had when she found that dead mouse in the laundry basket . . .

THAT'S . . .
  UMM . . .
NOT NICE.

Then I realized...

Oh no!

I **forgot** to take off the glasses, and they made me draw her **really badly**!

Oh man... What a way to start the day.

CHAPTER 4

When we got to the **zoo**, the first animals we saw were the **monkeys**.

I love monkeys, so me and Granddad went right up close to the fence.

I thought Granddad's monkey ears looked **silly**, but the monkeys must have thought they looked **real**, because the first thing that happened was

a monkey

threw a banana

right at Granddad!

Granddad *ducked* out of the way.

Then I ducked out of the way.

And the **banana** hit Henry . . .

right in the face!

It was **sooo funny**, I started laughing.

HAHA!!!!!!!!

I was laughing

so hard

I didn't see the second banana that was thrown.

Bella ducked it.

Blake ducked it.

Toby Hogan ducked it.

And it hit **me**
right on the side
of the head!

Now **everyone** was laughing at **me**!

Even Granddad!

HA HA HA HA HA HA

I guess it looked **pretty funny**!

As Henry and me stood there **flicking** the banana off ourselves, a whole bunch of **ducks** ran up to eat the bits off the ground.

They were funny, those ducks. Fat ones, skinny ones, and a big spotty one.

The **spotty** one had three little ducklings following it,

which was **very cute**.

Bella gave me a **hanky** to wipe myself. "Here you go, Weir," she said.

"Thanks," I said. And that's when I realized the hanky had little frogs on it.

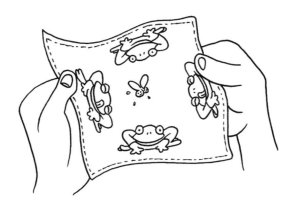

I looked up, and Bella was smiling.

Soon it was lunchtime, which was perfect, because I had heaps of ideas for **cool animal pictures**. First I tried a

giraffe and a **kangaroo**.

A Giraffaroo!

A **zebra** and an **elephant** . . .

A Zelephant!

A **panda** and a **gorilla** . . .

A Pandarilla!

But then I decided I wanted to try another
drawing of Bella. I quickly drew her while
she watched Henry

pretending he was a

sea lion.

OOOo!

OOOO!

I was pretty happy with my drawing and knew Bella would like it much more than the last one.

But as I went to hand it to her,

the skinny duck waddled over and

 snatched it

away from me! ⟫⟫⟫

HEY, DUCK!
THAT'S MINE!

Before I knew it, Bella had jumped up and was chasing after the duck with my drawing in its bill!

I ran after her.

I might have mentioned that I'm <u>not</u> a very fast runner . . .

And it turns out that duck was a
very fast waddler! **》》》》**

We chased that duck down past
the **gorilla** enclosure, **》》》》**

through the **bat** cave, >>>>

along the **penguin** pool . . . >>>>

But then we lost the duck around
the **meerkat** bend.

Not only had we lost the duck,
but now <u>we were lost</u>, too!

We couldn't find Granddad, Miss Franklin,
or anyone from school . . .

so we found **the next BEST thing . . .**

"Hey," said Bella, "what are you going to wear to **my party**?"

Huh? I thought to myself.

YOU KNOW IT'S A DRESS-UP PARTY, DON'T YOU?

"Oh yeah," I replied. "Sure . . . I'm going to go as . . ."

A FROG!

COOL!

"So what was your drawing of, anyway?" asked Bella.

"Oh, nothing," I replied. "Just an—"

"BELLA ALLEN!" the zoo loudspeaker suddenly boomed.

BELLA ALLEN, PLEASE RETURN TO THE ZOO KIOSK TO MEET YOUR TEACHER, MISS FRANKLIN.

"AND WEIRDO!" the loudspeaker continued.

HAS ANYONE SEEN A WEIRDO? HE WAS LAST SEEN WEARING A BLUE SHIRT, GRAY SHORTS, AND HIS BIG SISTER'S SHOES. COULD WEIRDO PLEASE RETURN TO THE MONKEY ENCLOSURE?

Everyone at the zoo laughed.

All the animals, too.

The monkeys . . .

The **penguins** . . .

Even the **duck** with the **glasses**!

I wanted to run away and hide, but before I could make a move, Granddad appeared.

I KNEW I'D FIND YOU NEAR THE FROGS!

The day at the zoo

wasn't a <u>complete</u> disaster.

On my way out, I found the *perfect* **birthday present** for Bella in the gift shop . . .

TWO
ROBOTS

At school the next day, Miss Franklin told us that we all needed to draw a picture of someone else in the class.

Here was my chance to draw Bella again!

But then Bella asked Henry if he would be her partner!

HENRY.

HENRY.

HENRY!!!

So I wound up with Clare instead . . .

I thought I'd done a

, pretty good job '

of my   drawing .

Henry's drawing of Bella was even worse than mine from the bus!

After school, Henry invited me over to his place to work on our costumes for Bella's party.

Henry was going as a **computer**. He put a box on his head, and I helped him attach a keyboard to his chest. When we finished, he looked like a human iPad.

He had lots of green cardboard for me to use to make a frog hat.

Perfect!

When we were finished, Henry showed me his COLLECTION OF ROCKS that he'd made to look like things . . .

. . . and then he introduced me to his sister.

"**WEIRDO?**" said Jane. "That's not very nice."

"Oh, no, that's his name," said Henry.

"Yeah, it's actually my name," I said.

WEIRD, ISN'T IT?

Then I met Henry's twin brothers. They looked <u>exactly</u> the same!

"I can see that," I said.

They even **talked** the same.

PEOPLE SAY
THEY CAN'T TELL
US APART.

PEOPLE SAY
THEY CAN'T TELL
US APART.

I couldn't tell them apart!

WE ARE DIFFERENT IN SOME WAYS, THOUGH.

WE ARE DIFFERENT IN SOME WAYS, THOUGH.

HE LIKES TO EAT GREEN M&M'S,
AND I LIKE TO EAT BLUE M&M'S.

YEAH, HE LIKES TO EAT BLUE M&M'S, AND I LIKE TO EAT GREEN M&M'S.

It was like looking at **two robots**.

Then Henry's mom and dad and their dog came out.

So this is what a <u>normal</u> **family** looks like!

"It's dinnertime, boys," said Mr. O'Henry.
"Come join us at the table."

My mom's and dad's dinners never
look how they're supposed to.

How
spaghetti is
supposed
to look.

How Mom's
spaghetti
looks.

How a Sunday dinner is supposed to look.

How Dad's Sunday dinner looks.

How noodles are supposed to look.

How Granddad's "noodles" look.

. . . but they always taste delicious!

But Mrs. O'Henry's roast looked just like the picture in the book!

YUUUUUM!

This is going to be SUPER yummy, I thought to myself.

Shame it **tasted** like **cardboard**!

CHAPTER 6

Today is Bella's **birthday party**!

Bella's present is
wrapped . . .

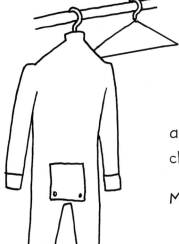

and my **green**
clothes are ready . . .

My **frog** hat is—

"**HEY**," I said, "where's my frog hat?"

Then I heard a

TERRIBLE

Where my frog hat SHOULD have been!

SPLASH!

coming from the **bathroom**.

ROGER!

NOOOOO

I ran to the bathroom, but it was too late.
My frog hat was already

sinking

in

bathwater . . .

I fished it out, and it

fell apart

in my hands.

I looked at Roger . . .

CLEAN!

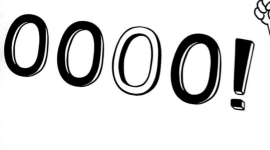
OOOO!

WEIR,
YOU CAN STILL
WEAR YOUR
GREEN
PAJAMAS.

"I can't just wear green," I complained. "I'll look like a **BIG** cucumber!"

Great, I get invited to Bella's party, and now I can't even go . . .

Then Sally stepped into the bathroom with an "excellent idea."

I HAVE AN EXCELLENT IDEA!

She pointed to the piles and piles of
toilet paper rolls in the corner.

Sally is supposed to be the clever one,
but this was the

worst idea ever!

"Sally, I'm <u>not</u> going as toilet paper!" I said.

Sally groaned. "No, we can wrap you with it, like a mummy!"

She picked up a roll and started spinning me around and around and around . . . and when I finally stopped whirling, I looked in the mirror and saw . . .

a really

COOL

mummy!

"Not bad," I said. "Thanks!"

So we're finally on our way to Bella's place, when we start

running out of gas.

But instead of stopping at the first gas station we see, Dad wants to wait until we come across a **cheaper** one!

Sometimes Dad can be **just as thrifty** as Mom!

Can you guess what happened next?

We ran out of gas!

So Dad orders us all out, to help push ⟫⟫⟫ the car, while Granddad runs off to get us a can of gas.

First my frog hat gets destroyed, then our car runs out of gas on our way to the party . . .

What could be worse?

RAIN!

Rain could be worse!

Granddad came back with gas, just as the rain stopped. But I no longer looked like a mummy . . .

I looked like a kid who'd been

FLUSHED down the toilet!

And my hands were covered in

FINKLES!

"What now?" I asked my genius sister.

DON'T ASK ME!

I climbed back into the car. I looked in the trunk behind me and saw the mega bag of **chips** and the huge pack of **safety pins** that Roger had snuck into Mom's cart.

Roger's shopping had just given me

a BRILLIANT idea!

SNABBIT!

CHAPTER 7

I turned myself into a **vending machine**!

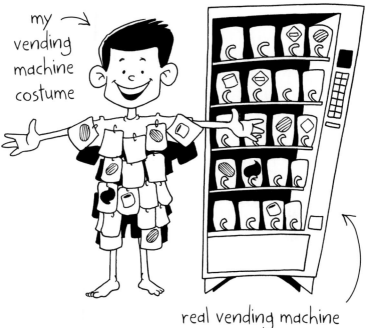

my vending machine costume

real vending machine

Everyone <u>loved it</u>, especially Bella's mom. She'd forgotten to pick up all the **party snacks**, so I'd arrived at just the right time . . .

The only downside was that Toby Hogan tried to **pay for the chips** by putting a **coin** in my **ear**...

There was supposed to be a **magician** at the party, but he couldn't come because his **rabbit** had **eaten** his car keys.

But that didn't matter too much, because there was something at the party that turned out to be **much more fun** than a magician.

My crazy, <u>weird</u> family.

Granddad was up first to do some tricks. He pulled out his teeth . . .

I CAN MAKE MY TEETH DISAPPEAR!

Then he made them _ _ _ _ _ _ ! ←vanish

WOW!

Next, he said,

WATCH MY MAGIC ELBOW.

Then **Dad** was up.

I NEED A
SODA

UH-OH.

I started to **panic**. What was he going to do?

Dad burped his way through

HAPPY BIRTHDAYYYYY

Then some **music** came on the radio and
Dad started doing his

<u>horsey</u> dance.

Roger

Soon  EVERYONE was joining in.

Bella

Me

Granddad

Mom

Dad

Next, **Sally** started making some **cool balloon animals** for everyone.

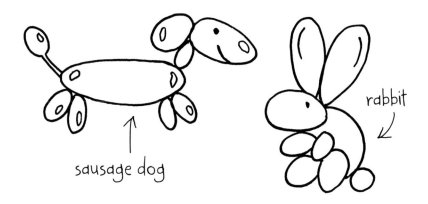

sausage dog

rabbit

Then I made the only **balloon animal** that I knew how to.

IT'S A SNAKE!

snake

134

Then I came up with

another GREAT idea!

I tied **my snake** to **Sally's rabbit** and made a **super-cool** animal.

snabbit

A SNABBIT!

THE
BEST

It was turning out to be a **great party**! I did a **BIG** drawing and we had a game of

pin the tail on the **donkey-potamus**

Roger helped Bella blow out her birthday candles, and Granddad laughed so loudly that his teeth

flew out

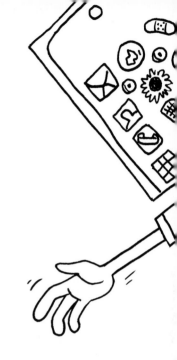

and landed in...

the candy bowl.

Henry thought they were **candy teeth**
and was just about to **grab** them, when I
scooped them up. "HENRY!
 HENRY!!
 HENRY!!!" I said.

"Huh?"

"Believe me, they're **NOT** as tasty as they look!"

Boy, that was close!

But before long, everyone was taking their **balloon animals** and saying goodbye.

Then I spotted Roger dropping leftover cake into the fruit juice.

CLEAN!

I was trying to **scoop** the cake out, when Bella came up to us.

"He is **soooooo** cute," said Bella.

Cute? Roger?

I handed him to Mom.

"I'm really glad you came to my party, Weir," Bella added. "You know, your drawing of Clare yesterday was really nice."

"Thanks," I said.

"You drew me, on the bus, but I guess I'm not as nice-looking as her . . ."

HUH?
OH NO, YOU ARE!
I JUST . . .
IT WAS . . .

THE PROBLEM WAS
YOUR GLASSES . . .

OH, YOU DON'T LIKE MY GLASSES?

NO, NO, I WAS WEARING YOUR GLASSES

... THAT'S WHY I DREW YOU FUNNY. I COULDN'T SEE PROPERLY!

"Oh!" said Bella.

"Hey, I almost forgot to give you this," I said, remembering the present in my pocket that I'd found for her at the zoo.

First, Bella opened the card I'd made her.

Bella blushed and gave me a **great big smile**.

I'm a bit short and I can't run very fast, but I'm **lucky** I can draw.

She opened the present next.

"Thanks, Weir," she said. "You're the best. And thanks for saving my party. It looked like it was going to be a disaster . . .

...UNTIL YOU AND YOUR FAMILY SHOWED UP.

Phew. I'd made it through my first birthday party with my new friends.

And the seventh-best-looking girl in school just called me

THE BEST.

Me!

Weir Do!

MORE
TO COME!

For my three **boys**

who helped me with
this book . . .

FROM
ANH

★ Henry's **funny-looking**
mum and dad, based on
drawings by **Xavier Do**

★ Henry's **strange** twin brothers,
based on drawings by **Luc Do**

★ **Blockhead** the parrot's crazy
habits, suggested by **Leon Do**